Graphic Organizers in Science™

Learning About the Effects of Natural Events with Graphic Organizers

Diana Estigarribia

The Rosen Publishing Group's
PowerKids Press™
New York

For my parents, Concepción and Augusto, with love

Published in 2005 by The Rosen Publishing Group, Inc.
29 East 21st Street, New York, NY 10010

First Edition

Editor: Natashya Wilson
Book Design: Mike Donnellan

Photo Credits: Cover, p. 8 © Weatherstock/Warren Faidley; p. 12 © Piotr Powietrzynski/Index Stock Imagery; p. 20 © Gary Conner/Index Stock Imagery.

Library of Congress Cataloging-in-Publication Data

Estigarribia, Diana.
Learning about the effects of natural events with graphic organizers / Diana Estigarribia.— 1st ed.
    p. cm. — (Graphic organizers in science)
Summary: Uses texts and graphs to explain the impact of storms, earthquakes, wildfires, and other natural disasters on Earth and those who live here.
ISBN 1-4042-2804-7 (lib. bdg.) — ISBN 1-4042-5038-7 (pbk.)
1. Graphic methods—Juvenile literature. 2. Natural disasters—Juvenile literature. [1. Graphic methods. 2. Natural disasters.] I. Title. II. Series.

QA90.E78 2005
363.34—dc22

                                    2003022448

Manufactured in the United States of America

T 5739

Contents

Concept Web: Natural Events

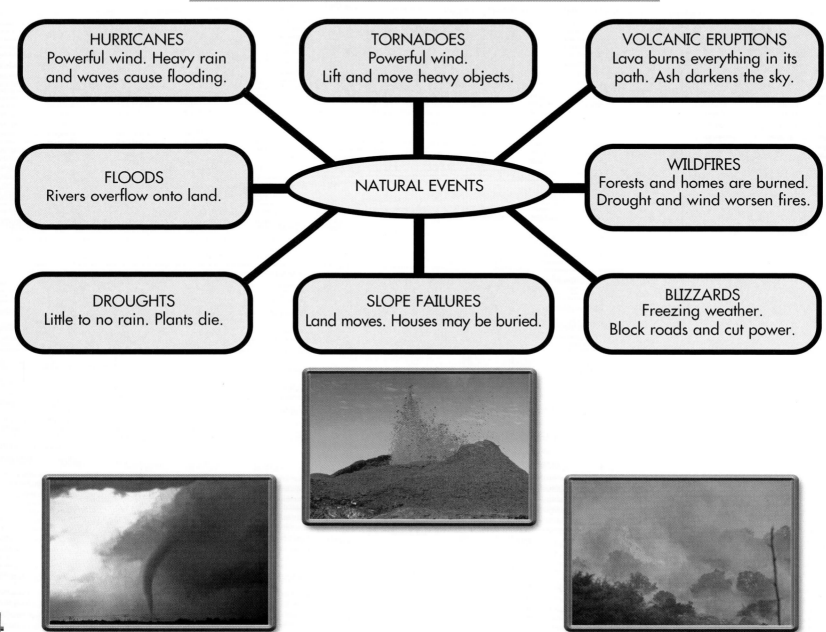

HURRICANES
Powerful wind. Heavy rain and waves cause flooding.

TORNADOES
Powerful wind.
Lift and move heavy objects.

VOLCANIC ERUPTIONS
Lava burns everything in its path. Ash darkens the sky.

FLOODS
Rivers overflow onto land.

NATURAL EVENTS

WILDFIRES
Forests and homes are burned. Drought and wind worsen fires.

DROUGHTS
Little to no rain. Plants die.

SLOPE FAILURES
Land moves. Houses may be buried.

BLIZZARDS
Freezing weather.
Block roads and cut power.

Forces of Nature

Natural events are forces of nature. Hurricanes, tornadoes, and earthquakes are just a few natural events that show Earth is an active planet. Natural events happen throughout the world. Sometimes natural events put people's lives in danger. They can cause injuries and loss of life and can destroy homes and the environment. When these things happen, the event is called a natural **disaster**. Natural events such as earthquakes and volcanic **eruptions** are caused by forces that shape Earth. Other natural events are caused by weather. Natural events can occur at any time. Being prepared for them can help people to stay safe.

Graphic organizers are written tools that organize facts. You can use them to study almost any subject. In this book, graphic organizers help you to learn about the effects of natural events.

Top: *This graphic organizer is called a concept web. The subject of the web goes in the middle. Elements and facts about the subject are written around it. More facts can be added as they are learned. This concept web shows different types of natural events.*
Bottom: *Tornadoes (left), volcanic eruptions (center), and wildfires (right) are natural events.*

Hurricanes and Tornadoes

Hurricanes and tornadoes are strong storms. A hurricane forms over warm ocean water and travels to land. It brings heavy rain, huge waves, and winds that blow up to 180 miles per hour (300 km/h). Hurricanes can be hundreds of miles (km) wide. Tornadoes are much smaller but are just as strong. They can form from thunderstorms that are over land. A tornado's funnel can carry heavy things hundreds of feet (m). Winds in the funnel may blow more than 300 miles per hour (483 km/h). Hurricanes and tornadoes have some similar effects on the environment. Both storms unsettle the balance of **ecosystems**. Their winds tear up buildings, trees, and land and can overturn cars. Heavy rains in both storms cause floods. The storms can destroy animal **habitats**, forcing the animals to find new homes and new sources of food.

Making a compare/contrast chart can help you to learn how two or more subjects compare, or are similar, and how they contrast, or are different. Here, facts about wind speed, area affected, and effects on the environment are listed for both hurricanes and tornadoes. These storms can cause a lot of harm. However, they also have some good effects.

Compare/Contrast Chart: Hurricanes and Tornadoes

	Hurricanes	Tornadoes
Wind Speed	Up to 180 miles per hour (300 km/h)	More than 300 miles per hour (483 km/h)
Area Affected	Islands and places on and near coasts. Hurricanes can affect hundreds of miles (km) of coastal areas.	Most common inland in the United States and Australia. Tornadoes affect a narrow path of land but the path can be about 1 mile (1.6 km) wide and 200 miles (322 km) long.
Effects on the Environment	Tear up trees and plants and flatten buildings. Wear away soil and sand. Flood land and may cause sewers to overflow, dirtying land and water supplies. Destroy animal habitat. Can kill people and animals. Under water, hurricane waves may harm ocean creatures. As the earth recovers, different types of trees and plants may grow back, making healthy changes to the forest and to underwater areas.	Tear up trees, plants, and buildings. Can lift and carry heavy things, including cars, animals, and people, for many feet (m). Can kill people and animals. The path of destruction is much narrower than that of a hurricane. However, a tornado can still cause changes to the amount and types of trees and plants growing in an area. This can help the environment.

Cause-and-Effect Chart: Floods

Floods in southeast Arizona *(top)* and eastern Mexico *(bottom)* destroyed houses and power lines and washed away land.

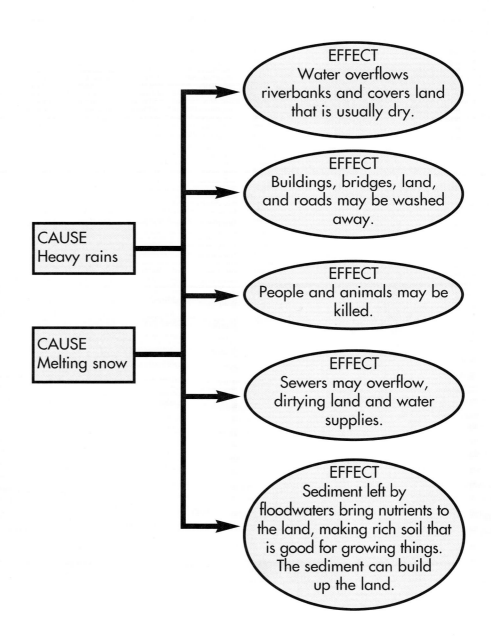

CAUSE
Heavy rains

CAUSE
Melting snow

EFFECT
Water overflows riverbanks and covers land that is usually dry.

EFFECT
Buildings, bridges, land, and roads may be washed away.

EFFECT
People and animals may be killed.

EFFECT
Sewers may overflow, dirtying land and water supplies.

EFFECT
Sediment left by floodwaters bring nutrients to the land, making rich soil that is good for growing things. The sediment can build up the land.

Floods

Floods happen when storms or melting snow create too much water for streams to hold. Extra water flows onto land that is usually dry. A **floodplain** is an area around a stream that floods when the stream's waters rise. Floodplains often have **fertile** soil, because floods bring **nutrients** to the ground. Floods also leave **sediment** behind, which builds up land. Floodplains may include damp areas called **wetlands**, which are home to many animals and plants. Wetlands help to control floods. They hold extra water and slow down floods. Because of the good soil and water supply, people have built towns on floodplains. They build dams to block water flow. This dries up wetlands and makes flooding worse. Dry land is washed away more easily than wetlands are. Floods can destroy buildings and can kill people and animals.

This is a cause-and-effect chart. Making a cause-and-effect chart will help you to learn the effects, or things that happen, because of a certain cause, or event. The cause happens first. The effects follow. This cause-and-effect chart is about floods. The worst flood of the twentieth century occurred in 1900 in Galveston, Texas. It killed more than 6,000 people.

Droughts

A drought is a period of dry weather with less rain or other moisture than usual. Droughts affect people, plants, and animals. Crops die, causing a food shortage or even **starvation**. Farmers cannot feed farm animals. Farmers may use water from wells to make up for the lack of rain, causing **groundwater** supplies to dry up. Wildfires may burn out of control. Dry soil creates dust problems. Plants and trees dry out and are more likely to be killed by insects that feed on them. Rivers and lakes dry up, causing fish and wildlife either to die or to move. Droughts can have some good effects. If a polluted lake dries up, people can clean up the dirty sediment at the bottom. Animals whose food comes from streams and lakes may find food faster when water levels are low. However, overall, droughts do more harm than good.

Making a timeline can help you to study history. A timeline arranges a series of events in the order in which they happened. This timeline is about droughts that happened in the United States. The earliest event is at the top. The most recent is at the bottom.

Timeline: Droughts in the United States

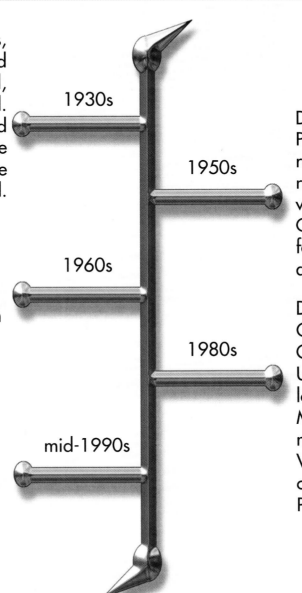

Drought hits Oklahoma, Texas, Colorado, New Mexico, and Kansas. Wind blows away the soil, leaving dusty, unfarmable land. Thick clouds of dust and sand called black blizzards darken the air for days at a time. People move away to find jobs and food.

Drought hits the northeastern United States. Many communities must use less water. Pollution becomes a problem in the water, because there is less water to wash pollutants away. Powerful wildfires burn in 1963.

In 1995, drought hits Texas and New Mexico and then moves into Arizona, California, Nevada, Utah, Colorado, Oklahoma, and Kansas. Wildfires burn in Texas, Oklahoma, and Kansas. Wheat and other crops are hurt. People are forced to use less water.

1930s

1950s

1960s

1980s

mid-1990s

Drought begins in the Great Plains area and eventually reaches from coast to coast. Low rainfall and unusually hot weather cause the drought. Grass used for cattle dries up, forcing ranchers to feed cactus and molasses to cows.

Drought begins on the West Coast and moves through the Great Plains to the eastern United States. Crops die. The low water level of the Mississippi River affects the moving of goods by boat. Wildfires burn millions of acres of forest. Half of Yellowstone Park in Wyoming is burned.

The blizzard of 1996 was one of the biggest winter storms in U.S. history. Philadelphia, Boston, New York, and other states got almost 2 feet (.6 m) of snow, causing airports, schools, and businesses to close for days.

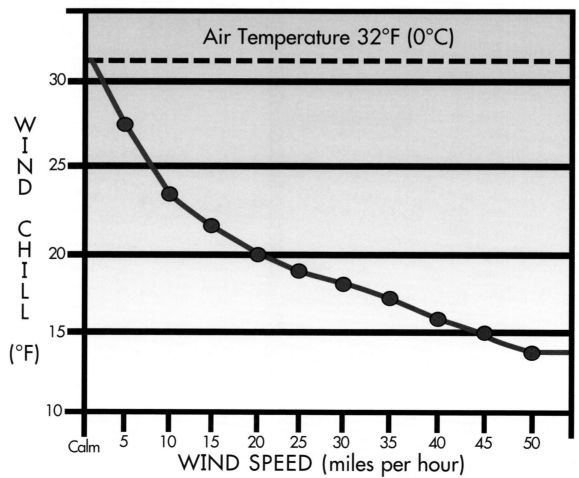

Air Temperature 32°F (0°C)

WIND CHILL (°F)

WIND SPEED (miles per hour)

Winter Weather

In some places winter brings **blizzards**, ice, and cold weather. A blizzard is a heavy snowstorm with strong winds. During a blizzard, snow piles up, burying cars and blocking roads. Businesses may do poorly because they have no customers. Communities must pay to have snow removed from roads and parking lots. Snow and ice may fall on power lines, causing blackouts. Communities may go without power for days while repairs are made. People can get **hypothermia** or **frostbite**. These are sicknesses caused by cold **temperatures**. Cold can also harm animals. Snow covers up the plants that animals eat, forcing them to move or starve. Floods may happen when the snow melts. However, the melted snow also becomes water for drinking water supplies and plant growth.

A line graph shows you how a change in one thing affects another thing. This line graph shows how wind speed affects wind chill. The red dots mark the wind chill at different wind speeds. When the air is calm, the temperature you feel outside is the same as the air temperature. However, if the wind is blowing, to you the temperature will feel colder.

Slope Failures

A slope failure is the downhill movement of soil, rock, mud, and other matter. Slope failures happen when heavy rain or snow, earthquakes, or construction loosen earth. **Gravity** then pulls matter downward. Slope failures can move slowly or quickly. Landslides are large amounts of rocks and earth that slip down a slope. Rock and soil falling from cliffs or steep slopes is called a fall. **Mudflows** move fast, turning soil into a flowing river of mud that can bury towns and kill people. **Avalanches** are masses of snow and ice that slide down mountains. Slope failures have bad and good effects. They can destroy buildings and bury people and animals. They can block streams and roads. They may pollute water supplies. However, they can also create new paths, shelters, and mating places for animals.

Making a Venn diagram can teach you how related things are alike and how they are different. This Venn diagram compares mudflows (green), avalanches (red), and landslides (blue). The features that all three share go in the middle. The features that belong to only one go in the outer areas. The features that two share go in the area between those two.

Venn Diagram: Slope Failures

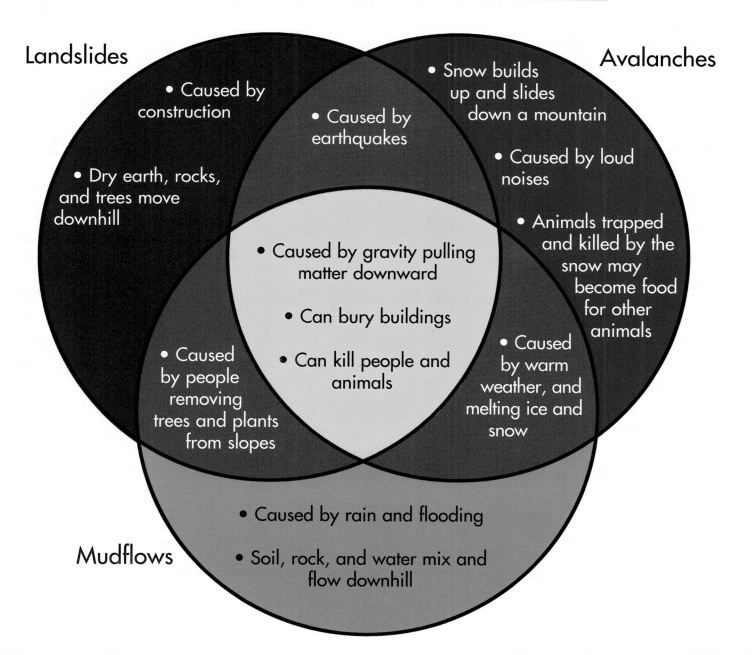

Landslides

- Caused by construction
- Dry earth, rocks, and trees move downhill

Avalanches

- Snow builds up and slides down a mountain
- Caused by loud noises
- Animals trapped and killed by the snow may become food for other animals

- Caused by earthquakes

- Caused by gravity pulling matter downward
- Can bury buildings
- Can kill people and animals

- Caused by people removing trees and plants from slopes

- Caused by warm weather, and melting ice and snow

Mudflows

- Caused by rain and flooding
- Soil, rock, and water mix and flow downhill

15

Chart: Volcanic Eruptions

Volcano	Location	Year	Deaths	Effects
Tambora	Indonesia	1815	92,000	Cold spring and summer in 1816, with snow and frost in New England and Europe. Many crops are destroyed worldwide, causing people to die of hunger. Glaciers move down mountains to very low areas.
Krakatau	Indonesia	1883	36,000	The island of Krakatau is blown apart. Two-thirds of it falls into the sea. Tsunamis flood nearby islands, killing many people. World temperature averages fall. Dust and gas from the volcano affect the colors of the sky around the world.
Mount Pelée	Martinique	1902	29,000	Hot gas and ash hit the town of Saint-Pierre, killing all but two people. About one month later another blast of gas and ash destroy the town of Morne Rouge. The blasts of gas and ash are called pyroclastic flows.
Mount Saint Helens	United States	1980	57	The largest known landslide in history slides off the top of the mountain. The nearby Silver Lake area is destroyed. Even today, hunting and fishing are not back to normal. Crops in eastern Washington are very good in 1981.
Pinatubo	Philippines	1991	800	Earthquakes shake the ground. Nearly 100,000 homes are destroyed. Sulfur dioxide gas fills the air around earth, lowering average temperatures around the world for a few years, causing worse floods and droughts than usual.

Volcanic Eruptions

Volcanoes are mountains that sometimes erupt. During an eruption, rocks and ash shoot into the air. Hot, liquid rock called **lava** pours down the mountainside. There are hundreds of active volcanoes on Earth. Many of them are part of the Ring of Fire, an area that circles the Pacific Ocean. Volcanic eruptions can cause huge waves called **tsunamis**, which may flood land. An eruption can affect the environment for years. Wind carries the ash around Earth. The tiny ash pieces block some sunlight, lowering Earth's average temperature slightly for 1 or 2 years. Hot gases and lava burn land and destroy buildings. They can kill people and wildlife. However, once they cool, the rock and the ash make a fertile soil that is good for growing crops. People can also use the heat from volcanoes for power in their homes.

This is a chart. Charts can be used to organize all kinds of facts. Here, facts about some of the best-known volcanic eruptions have been collected. Hot gas from a volcanic eruption can travel about 124 miles per hour (200 km/h). The temperature of lava can be from 1,112 to 2,192°F (600–1,200°C). Hardened lava can add new land to an area.

Earthquakes

Earthquakes happen when the giant **plates** that form Earth's surface bump and slide past one another. Earthquakes can cause slope failures. They may open cracks in the ground. Some earthquakes are warnings of a coming volcanic eruption. People who study earthquakes measure an earthquake's movement with a **seismograph**. An earthquake's strength is measured on the **Richter scale**. Measurements start at 1. Weak earthquakes may knock over objects. Powerful earthquakes may destroy roads, bridges, and buildings. They may break gas lines, which can start fires. Earthquakes also occur under the ocean floor, causing tsunamis. The most powerful earthquake of the twentieth century happened in Chile on May 22, 1960. It measured 9.5 on the Richter scale.

Making a KWL chart about a subject can help you to figure out what you need to study. In the first column, write down what you already know. In the middle column, write the questions to which you want to find answers. As you study, write down what you learn in the last column. This KWL chart shows some things you can learn about earthquakes.

KWL Chart: Earthquakes

What I Know	What I Want to Know	What I Have Learned
• Earthquakes shake the ground.	• What causes the ground to move?	• Earth's surface is made of huge plates of rock. When the edges of the plates rub together, the rock shakes. We feel the movement as earthquakes. Volcanic eruptions and bombs set off by humans can also cause earthquakes.
• There are weak and strong earthquakes.	• How do people decide how powerful an earthquake is?	• Seismographs make wavelike marks on paper that show how much the ground moved. The height of the marks is measured on the Richter scale. The bigger the wave mark is, the more powerful the earthquake was.
• People should get under a table or a doorway during an earthquake.	• What are other ways to stay safe during an earthquake?	• Stay inside unless there is a fire. If you are outside, move into an open area far from poles, buildings, and trees. If you are in a car, pull over and stay in the car. Pull over in as safe a place as possible, away from poles, buildings, and trees.

Cycle: Wildfires

Lightning, heat, or a spark begins a wildfire. Wildfires can also be started by people who are careless with matches or campfires outside.

Dead plants, dried pine needles and leaves, fallen tree branches, and other dry matter collect on the forest floor.

Fire burns up the dead matter on the forest floor, leaving ash behind. It kills some plants and animals. The heat causes some trees' pinecones to release seeds, which fall to the ground. Animals not killed by the fire move to new areas.

Ash becomes rich soil that is good for plant growth. New plants grow, starting with grasses and wildflowers and then trees. Animals return. Old plants whose roots lived through the fire grow again. Trees that were partly burned may grow again.

Wildfires

Any outdoor fire that is not controlled is called a wildfire. Wildfires burn up dead plants and trees, helping living trees and plants to grow better. Fires also kill pests and add nutrients to soil. Forests need wildfires for healthy growth. Some trees, such as the lodgepole pine, use the fire's heat to free their seeds. However, wildfires can also burn out of control. They can destroy homes and kill people and animals. Wildfires burn on the ground, under the soil, and along the tops of trees. They spread fast when it is windy. Lightning starts an average of 14,000 fires per year. These fires burn more than 2 million acres (8 million ha) of land. Wildfires can reach speeds of 15 miles per hour (29 km/h). Firefighters may set controlled fires to burn dead matter that could cause a larger fire later.

This graphic organizer is called a cycle. Cycles show events that happen over and over again in the same pattern. A cycle has no beginning and no end. This cycle shows the events of a wildfire. Wildfires destroyed almost 700,000 acres (283,280 ha) of land and nearly 1,500 homes in southern California in October 2003. About 20 people died.

Staying Safe

Although no one knows when the next natural event will happen, people can practice safety and can plan ahead. They can keep supplies ready, such as drinking water, first aid kits, canned food, nonelectric can openers, radios, flashlights, and batteries. Scientists can warn people when hurricanes, tornadoes, or winter storms might happen. To protect their homes before a hurricane or tornado, people cover the windows with wood. People in tornado areas may have storm cellars to go into for safety. Earthquakes, droughts, volcanic eruptions, and wildfires are harder to predict. People who live in places where these natural events occur can plan for them. Buildings can be built to last through an earthquake. Sometimes people must leave their homes for safer places during natural events. By being prepared for these events people have a good chance of staying safe.

Glossary

avalanches (A-vuh-lanch-ez) Large amounts of snow and ice that slide down mountains.

blizzards (BLIH-zurdz) Bad snowstorms with very strong winds.

disaster (dih-ZAS-ter) An event that causes suffering or loss.

ecosystems (EE-koh-sis-temz) Communities of living things and the areas in which they live.

eruptions (ih-RUP-shunz) Explosions of gases, smoke, or lava from volcanoes.

fertile (FER-tul) Good for making and growing things.

floodplain (FLUD-playn) Land around rivers that floods when water levels are high.

frostbite (FROST-byt) Harm to the body caused by freezing.

graphic organizers (GRA-fik OR-guh-ny-zerz) Charts, graphs, and pictures that sort facts and ideas and make them clear.

gravity (GRA-vih-tee) The natural force that causes objects to move toward the center of Earth.

groundwater (GROWND-wah-tur) Water that is found underground, where all of the air spaces in the soil and rock are filled with water.

habitats (HA-bih-tats) Surroundings where animals or plants naturally live.

hypothermia (hy-puh-THUR-mee-uh) An illness in which body heat becomes too low.

lava (LAH-vuh) A hot liquid made of melted rock that comes out of a volcano.

mudflows (MUD-flohz) Rivers of mud that flow quickly downhill.

nutrients (NOO-tree-ints) Foods that a living thing needs to live and to grow.

plates (PLAYTS) The moving pieces of Earth's crust, which is the top layer of Earth.

Richter scale (RIK-ter SKAYL) A tool that measures an earthquake's strength.

sediment (SEH-dih-ment) Gravel, sand, silt, or mud carried by wind or water.

seismograph (SYZ-muh-graf) A tool that measures movement in Earth's crust.

starvation (star-VAY-shun) The act of suffering or dying from hunger.

temperatures (tem-pruh-cherz) How hot or cold things are.

tsunamis (soo-NAH-meez) Huge waves caused by movements of Earth's crust.

wetlands (WET-landz) Land with a lot of moisture in the soil.

Index

A
avalanches, 14

B
blizzards, 13

D
droughts, 10, 22

E
earthquakes, 5, 18, 22
ecosystems, 6

F
floodplain, 9

floods, 9, 13

H
habitats, 6
hurricanes, 5–6

L
lava, 17

M
mudflows, 14

R
Richter scale, 18
Ring of Fire, 17

S
seismograph, 18
slope failures, 14

T
tornadoes, 5–6, 22
tsunamis, 17

V
volcanoes, 17

W
wetlands, 9
wildfires, 21–22

Web Sites

Due to the changing nature of Internet links, PowerKids Press has developed an online list of Web sites related to the subject of this book. This site is updated regularly. Please use this link to access the list:
www.powerkidslinks.com/gosci/naturalgo/